The Seasons of Little Wolf

Written by JONATHAN LONDON 🐾 Illustrated by JON VAN ZYLE

WESTWINDS
PRESS®

It's spring in the northern forests.
White Wolf digs a den
   deserted long ago
by foxes or wolverines.

It is time. She is ready.
As White Wolf curls up in her dark home,
Gray Wolf, her mate, stands guard outside.

In the morning,
four blind and fuzzy pups
   nuzzle, hungry for life . . .

and Gray Wolf howls his song of celebration.

At two weeks old, Little Wolf
opens his deep blue eyes.
He can see!
Hungry, he fills his belly
on mother's milk . . .

then bumbles outside
    for the very first time.
And three fat little bundles of fur
waddle after him.

It's time to play!

Wolf tag . . .

tug-of-war . . .

and hide-and-seek!

Little Wolf tumbles with Little Sister
    and their brothers
among the stones and wildflowers . . .

then climbs to the top.
King of the Mountain!

Little Wolf is a ball of energy!
   When Gray Wolf goes hunting,
Little Wolf wants to go with him.
But he's too small. He whines
and White Wolf stays behind to babysit.

When Little Wolf misbehaves,
   White Wolf picks him up
by the scruff of his neck
   and carries him off:

                   a wolf's time-out.

At last, Gray Wolf comes home
     and Little Wolf yaps and twists
and leads the swarm of pups
     as they nip at Gray Wolf's muzzle.
Tasty chunks of meat drop out
and the little ones chow down.

All through the warm months of summer,
the pups chase grasshoppers and butterflies.
Little Wolf leaps . . .
    and misses
and falls flat on his belly in the grass.

But one day, he stares at the ground—
his ears rammed forward, listening . . .

and *POUNCES!*

Little Wolf pins a deer mouse
between his paws.
His first real catch!

Finally, in the autumn,
when the leaves start to fall,
Little Wolf goes on his first *big* hunt.
Eyes now as yellow as the
birch leaves,
he lopes behind Gray Wolf and
White Wolf,
followed by Little Sister and
their brothers.
They float like ghost-
shadows
through the moonbeams.

Gray Wolf pauses,
    and sniffs the crisp night air.
There, on a rock spine against the sky,
    stands a bull moose—his huge rack
cradling the moon.

Suddenly, Bull Moose bolts—
    and the pack charges after him.
Bull Moose scrambles down a
    steep gully,
the wolves snapping
    at his heels.

He spins and kicks sharp,
    powerful hooves—

THWACK!

—and with a *yelp* Little Wolf goes flying.

Bull Moose thunders off
through quaking aspen.
Soon Gray Wolf gives up the chase
and turns back.

Little Wolf's body lies limp.

The trees seem to stand at attention
and hold their breath.
Gray Wolf sniffs and nudges Little Wolf.
  Little Sister whimpers.
White Wolf licks her little one's fur,
but he doesn't stir.

All is still.

Suddenly, Little Wolf's eyes
pop open! They glow
like precious stones.

He's *ALIVE! ALIVE!*

And the trees breathe
and sway in the breeze.
And Little Wolf's family
yaps and prances and rears up
in a wolf's dance of joy.

Months pass.
       Snows fall.
It's winter in the northern mountains
and food is scarce.

But after a good hunt,
Little Wolf joins his voice
with the others
   in the music of the wild.
It floats high
across the snowy mountains
and into the sky.

Someday he will lead a wolf pack
   of his own.

It will be the Season of Little Wolf.

AUTHOR'S NOTE

Wolf packs are similar to human families, normally with father and mother wolves as leaders of the pack, followed by uncles and aunts, brothers and sisters. Mother and father wolves usually mate for life. They lead the hunt, and defend the young ones from bull moose and bears, and their territory from other wolf packs.

Usually there are four to six pups in a litter, born in the spring. By the time the wolves are two or three years old, they generally feel the urge to leave the pack. A male will look for a mate, mark his own territory, and, in the spring, start a pack of his own.

Until the late 1800s, wolves could be seen or heard across much of North America and throughout Europe and northern Asia. But for more than 100 years, up until 1973, attempts were made in the United States, Canada, and northern Mexico to destroy wolves, rather than to learn to live with them. Wolves were brutally hunted, trapped, and poisoned to the brink of extinction, especially in the lower 48 states. In 1973, when the Endangered Species Act was introduced, there were practically no gray wolves left in the American West, and few in Minnesota and northern Michigan.

According to the Fish and Wildlife Service, around 6,000 wolves now live in the continental United States and 8,000 to 11,000 in Alaska. But proposals to remove Endangered Species Act protections might once again threaten their security in the wild. If this could be prevented, you, too, may someday hear Little Wolf's voice joined with his family's in "the music of the wild."

For Jon Van Zyle, artist of
the Wilderness
—J. L.

For these, and all future little wolves.
—J. V. Z.

Library of Congress
Cataloging-in-Publication Data
London, Jonathan, 1947-
    The seasons of Little Wolf / written by Jonathan London ; illustrated by Jon Van Zyle.
        pages cm
    Summary: Almost from the time they are born, Little Wolf enjoys playing with Sister Wolf and their brothers, but the pups are also learning from Gray Wolf and White Wolf about how to survive in the wild one day. Includes facts about wolves.
    ISBN 978-1-941821-06-0 (hardcover)
    1. Gray wolf—Juvenile fiction. [1. Gray wolf—Fiction. 2. Wolves—Fiction. 3. Animals—Infancy—Fiction.] I. Van Zyle, Jon, illustrator. II. Title.
    PZ10.3.L8534Se 2014
    [E]—dc23
                        2014012700

Editor: Michelle McCann
Designers: Vicki Knapton and
Jon Van Zyle

WestWinds Press®
An imprint of

GA
GRAPHIC ARTS
BOOKS®

P.O. Box 56118
Portland, OR 97238-6118
(503) 254-5591
www.graphicartsbooks.com

Printed in China